TEENY WITCH

Goes on
VACATION

by LIZ MATTHEWS
illustrated by CAROLYN LOH

Troll Associates

Library of Congress Cataloging-in-Publication Data

Matthews, Liz.
   Teeny Witch goes on vacation / by Liz Matthews; illustrated by
Carolyn Loh.
      p.   cm.
   Summary: When Teeny Witch and her three witch aunts cannot decide
where to spend their vacation, she satisfies them all by taking
three vacations in three different places.
    ISBN 0-8167-2278-1 (lib. bdg.)   ISBN 0-8167-2279-X (pbk.)
    [1. Vacations—Fiction. 2. Aunts—Fiction. 3. Witches—Fiction.]
I. Loh, Carolyn, ill. II. Title.
PZ7.M4337Th 1991
[E]—dc20   90-11141

"Where are we going on vacation?" asked Teeny Witch.
"Vacation time is a special time. A vacation should be
fun for everyone."

Teeny's three witch aunts didn't know what to do.
They were trying to decide where to go on vacation.
But each of them wanted to go to a different place.

"Let's go to the mountains," said Aunt Vicky. "We can sleep in a tent. We can fish in a lake. We can hike in the woods. It will be fun."

"I don't like the mountains," said Aunt Ticky. "The beach is the best vacation place. You can swim. You can make sand castles at the beach."

Aunt Icky sighed. "I do not like the mountains or the beach," she said. "I want to spend my vacation at home. Home is the best place to relax."

"Let's let Teeny decide," said Teeny's three aunts.
Teeny Witch was puzzled. Everyone wanted to go to a
different place. How could they all have fun? Teeny
Witch thought and thought. Then she smiled.

"I know where we should go," said Teeny Witch.
"Aunt Vicky should go to the mountains. Aunt Ticky
should go to the beach. And Aunt Icky should stay
home. That way everyone will have fun."

"But what about you, Teeny?" Aunt Icky asked.
"A vacation without Teeny Witch will not be fun," said Aunt Ticky.
"Who will you go with?" Aunt Vicky asked Teeny.

Teeny smiled. "I will have the best vacation of all," she said. "I like the mountains and the beach. I will spend part of my vacation at each place."

Teeny looked at Aunt Icky. Teeny really did not want to stay home for vacation. At home there was nothing to do. But she did not want to hurt Aunt Icky's feelings.

"I will stay home, too," said Teeny Witch. "I will spend the last part of my vacation at home with Aunt Icky."

The next day Aunt Vicky packed up her bumpity old pickup truck. She packed camping gear. She put in fishing gear, too. Teeny helped.

"Goodbye, Teeny," called Aunt Ticky. Aunt Ticky was packing up her little car. "I will see you at the beach."

"Goodbye, Teeny," shouted Aunt Icky. "Have fun at the mountains. Have fun at the beach, too. I will see you when you get home to vacation with me."

"Goodbye," said Teeny Witch. And she waved to Aunt Ticky and Aunt Icky.

Vroom! Aunt Vicky started the truck. Teeny waved and waved as the pickup truck drove away. Bumpity-bump-bump! Off toward the mountains they went.

Aunt Vicky and Teeny Witch drove a long way.
They bumpity-bumped up mountain roads.
They bumpity-bumped down mountain roads.

At last they stopped.
"Here we are!" shouted Aunt Vicky. "We will have lots of fun."

Teeny got out of the pickup truck. She looked around. There were mountains everywhere. There was a lake, too. It was very beautiful. It looked like a good place to spend a vacation.

Teeny and her aunt unpacked the old bumpity truck.
Then they set up camp. Up went a big old tent.
Out came the fishing gear.
   "Let's go fishing," said Aunt Vicky.
   And off to the lake they went.

"Look!" said Aunt Vicky. "There are lots of fish in the lake."

20   "Let's catch them!" called Teeny.

Splash! Splosh!
Into the water went
their fishing lines.
"I got one!" yelled
Aunt Vicky. She
pulled in her fishing
line. Splosh! Out
of the lake came an
old boot.

Teeny laughed. What a strange thing to catch!
Just then, Teeny's line jumped.

"I got one!" called Teeny. Splash! Splash! Teeny pulled
a funny little fish out of the lake. She smiled, and then
she decided to put the little fellow back.

"Fishing is fun," said Aunt Vicky. "But it is getting late. Let's go back to camp."

Soon it was dark. Teeny and Aunt Vicky went into the big, old tent to sleep. They laid their sleeping bags on the ground. The ground was bumpy.

Aunt Vicky liked bumpy things. She liked bumpy roads. She liked her bumpity truck. She liked the bumpy ground, too. Aunt Vicky went right to sleep.

Teeny Witch did not go to sleep. The ground was too bumpy to sleep on. And there were bugs in the tent. Buzz! Buzz! Buzz! went the bugs. Teeny did not like those buzzing bugs.

"Wake up, Aunt Vicky," called Teeny. "There are bugs in the tent."

"Bugs!" yelled Aunt Vicky. She sat up and smiled. "I will catch those bugs. I will put them in my ugly bug collection. This is the best vacation ever," she said.

Teeny Witch smiled. Some things about a mountain vacation were not fun. Teeny did not like the bumpy ground or the buzzing bugs. But she did like fishing.

"Sometimes a vacation is part good and part bad," Teeny said.

The mountain part of Teeny's vacation went by fast. Teeny did lots of things every day. She went fishing. She walked in the woods with Aunt Vicky. There was always something new to do.

Before long it was time to leave the mountains. It was time to go to the beach. Aunt Vicky drove Teeny to the beach. Aunt Ticky met them in her little pink car.

"Goodbye, Aunt Vicky," called Teeny Witch. "I had fun at the mountains." She waved as Aunt Vicky drove away.

"You will have fun at the beach, too," Aunt Ticky said to Teeny.

The next day Teeny went to the beach with
Aunt Ticky.

"I am going to make a sand castle," said Teeny Witch.
Teeny went down near the water. She made a big castle
out of sand.

"How do you like my sand castle?" Teeny asked.
"It is very nice," said Aunt Ticky. "But you made it
too close to the water."

Splash! A big wave rolled in. Water splashed over Teeny's castle. When the water rolled back out, the castle was gone.

"Oh well," Teeny said. "I will make a new one tomorrow."

The next day Teeny had fun, too. She played in the water. Splashing in the water was lots of fun.

At night Teeny and Aunt Ticky walked along the water. "The beach is very pretty at night," Teeny said.

Every day Teeny Witch had lots to do. But soon her beach vacation was over, too. It was time to vacation at home with Aunt Icky.

Teeny got into Aunt Ticky's little car. Vroom!
Off they drove toward home. The little car went fast.

Soon Teeny Witch was home again.
"Goodbye, Aunt Ticky," called Teeny Witch. Aunt
Ticky waved. Vroom! The car drove back to the beach.

"Did you have fun?" Aunt Icky asked Teeny. "Did you do lots of things?"

Teeny Witch nodded. "Every day I did lots of things at the mountains. And every day I did lots of things at the beach."

Aunt Icky hugged Teeny Witch. "Thank you for spending some vacation time with me," she said. "I know you did not want to vacation at home. There is nothing to do here but relax."

Teeny smiled. "At first I did not want to spend any of my vacation at home. But now I do. I want to relax."

Aunt Icky was puzzled. "Don't you want to have fun?"
she asked.

"I am tired of having fun," said Teeny Witch.
"I had too much fun. Now I need a vacation from
my vacations!"

Teeny Witch spent the rest of her vacation at home with Aunt Icky.

Every day they relaxed and spent time together.

Teeny told Aunt Icky all about her vacations. "I had
fun at the mountains," she said. "I had fun at the beach.
And now I am having fun here with you."

Teeny Witch smiled. "I guess the best way to have fun on vacation is to spend it with people you love!"